CW00854045

Little Miss Priss and Big Bear Paint the Walls

ISBN Softcover: 978-1-64318-032-8

Front Cover Image by Kilson Spany

Book Cover Design by Kilson Spany

Interior Layout Design by Kilson Spany

1097 N. 400th Rd

Baldwin City, KS, 66006

www.imperiumpublishing.com

Dedications

To my granddaughters, Kate Ralston (The real miss Priss),

and her sister Megan.

Little Miss Priss and Big Bear Paint The Wall

Written
By Linda Ralston

Illustrated
By Kilson Spany

Raindrops sounded tic tic tic on Little Miss Priss's bedroom window. When she woke from her nap, Big Bear was lying on her bed. "Oh, Big Bear, you're here. Let's draw a picture!" Everyone called her Little Miss Priss... you can probably guess why. Her grandmother, Bibbi, started calling her that name and the name stuck like peanut butter on the roof of your mouth.

Big Bear was special because no one else could see or hear him except Miss Priss. He was big and had a goofy grin. They played together every day. Big Bear had wonderful ideas about things to do. Sometimes, however, Big Bear's ideas got Miss Priss into trouble.

"I would love to draw a picture", said Big Bear. He grabbed the markers that Bibbi had given Miss Priss for Christmas.

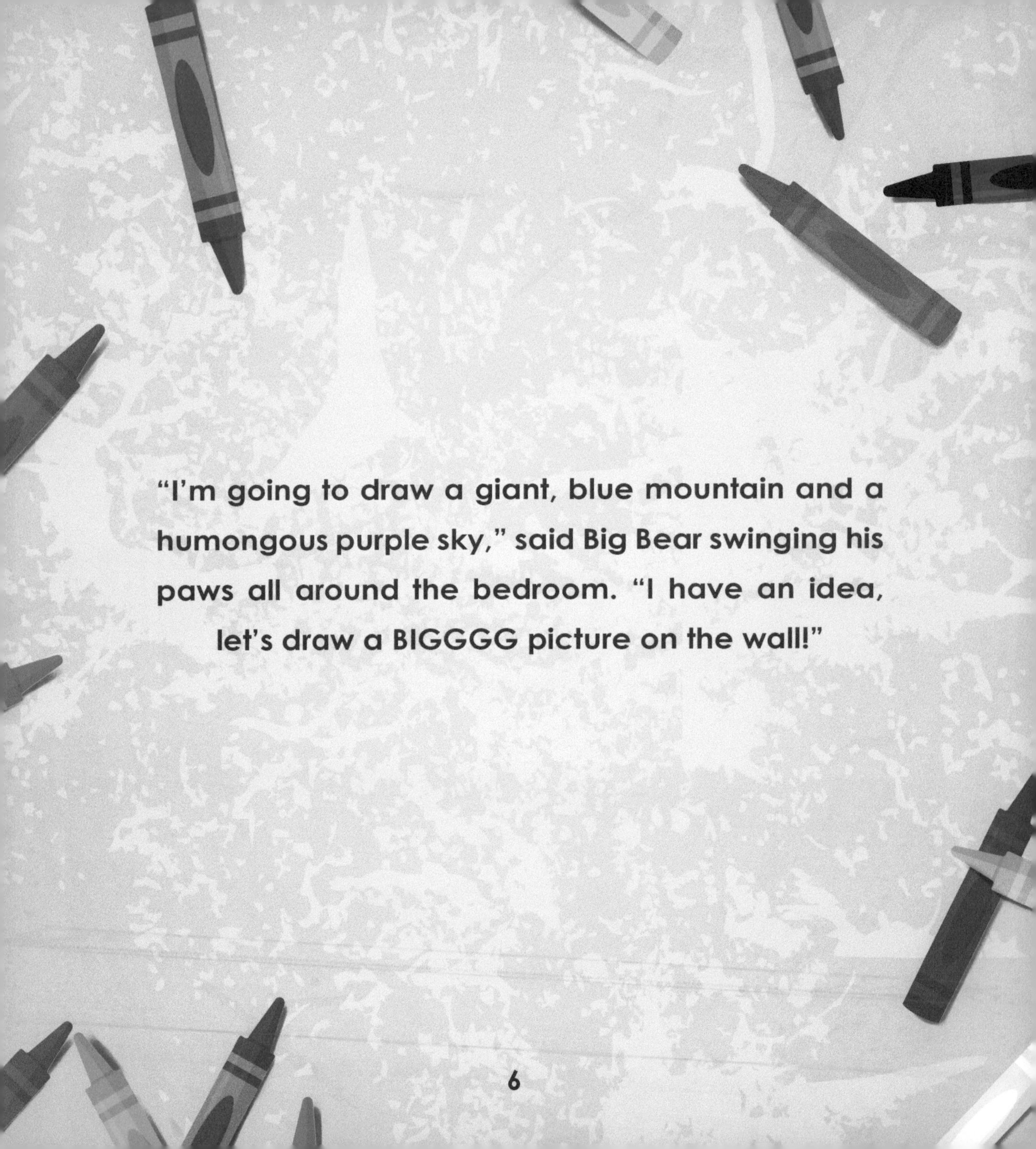

"I'm going to draw a giant, blue mountain and a humongous purple sky," said Big Bear swinging his paws all around the bedroom. "I have an idea, let's draw a BIGGGG picture on the wall!"

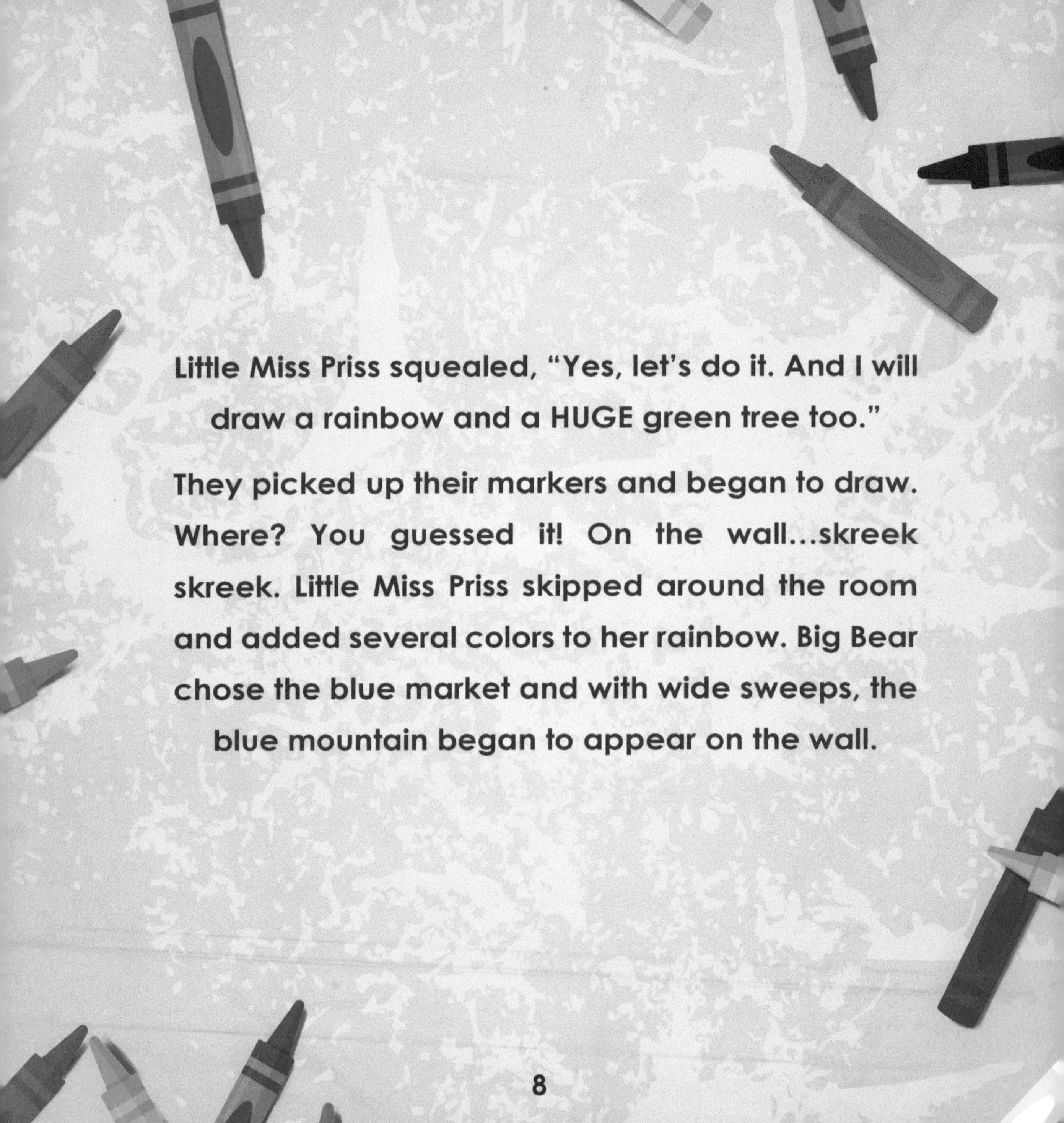

Little Miss Priss squealed, “Yes, let’s do it. And I will draw a rainbow and a HUGE green tree too.”

They picked up their markers and began to draw. Where? You guessed it! On the wall…skreek skreek. Little Miss Priss skipped around the room and added several colors to her rainbow. Big Bear chose the blue market and with wide sweeps, the blue mountain began to appear on the wall.

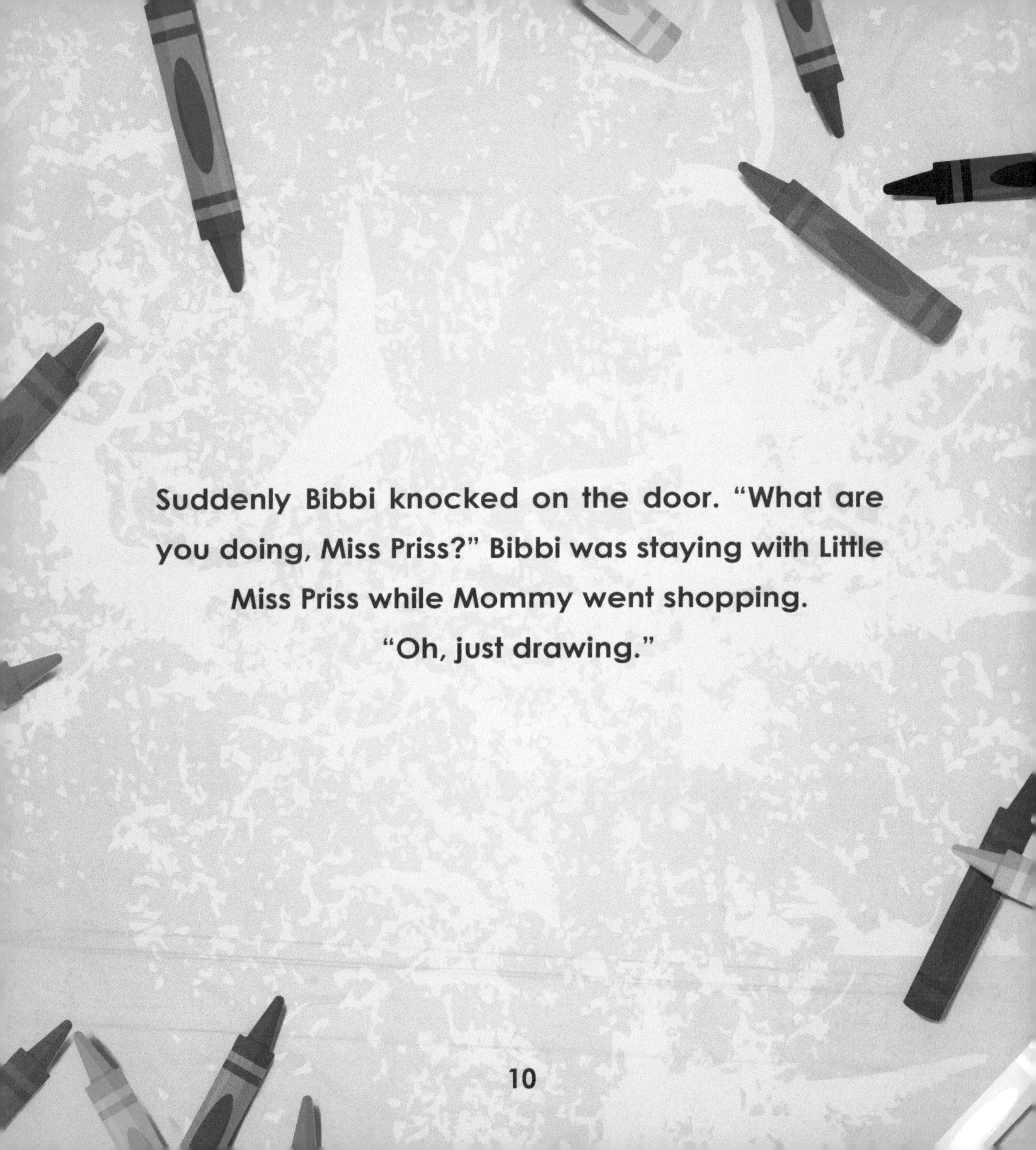

Suddenly Bibbi knocked on the door. “What are you doing, Miss Priss?” Bibbi was staying with Little Miss Priss while Mommy went shopping.

“Oh, just drawing.”

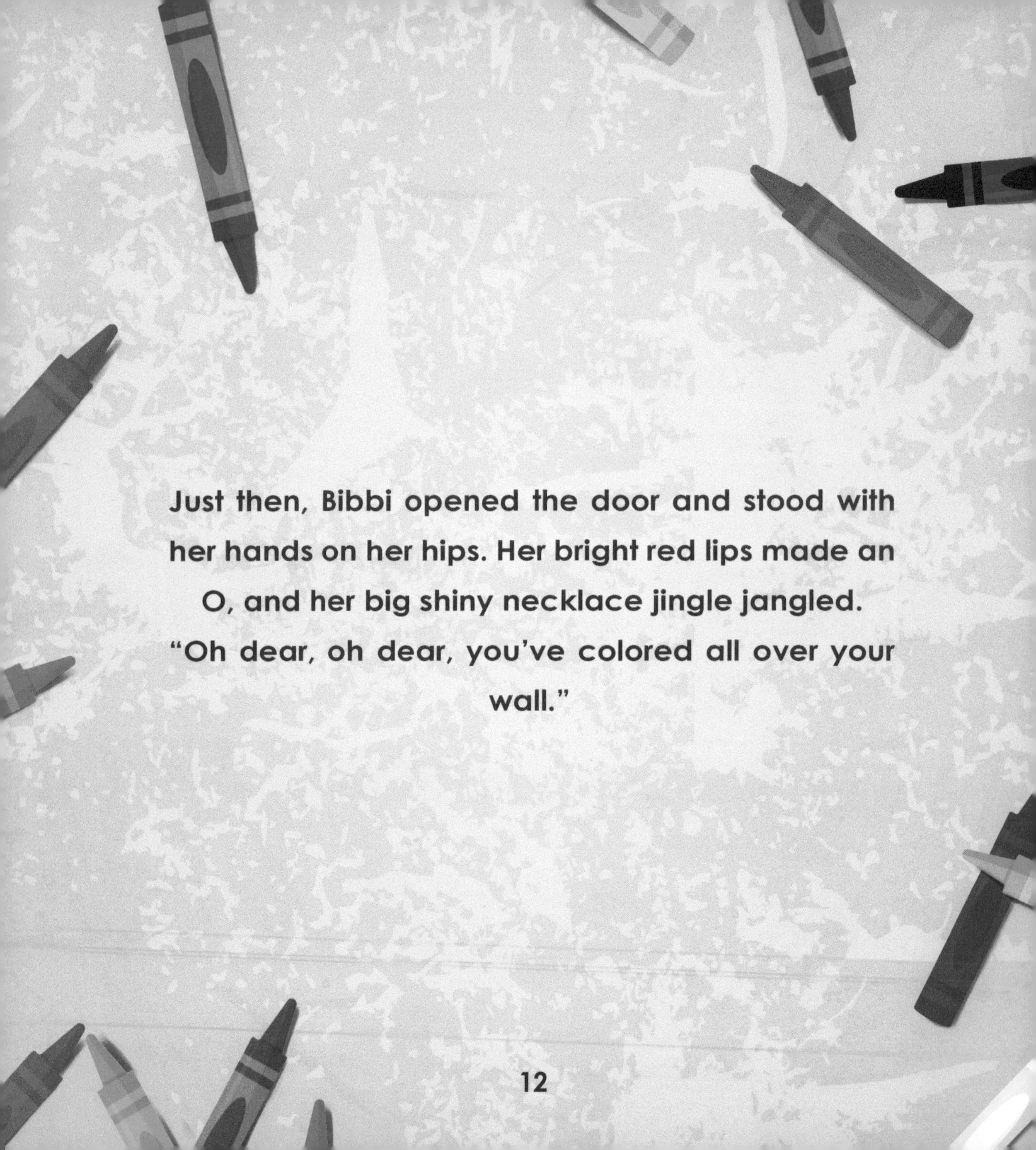

Just then, Bibbi opened the door and stood with her hands on her hips. Her bright red lips made an O, and her big shiny necklace jingle jangled. “Oh dear, oh dear, you’ve colored all over your wall.”

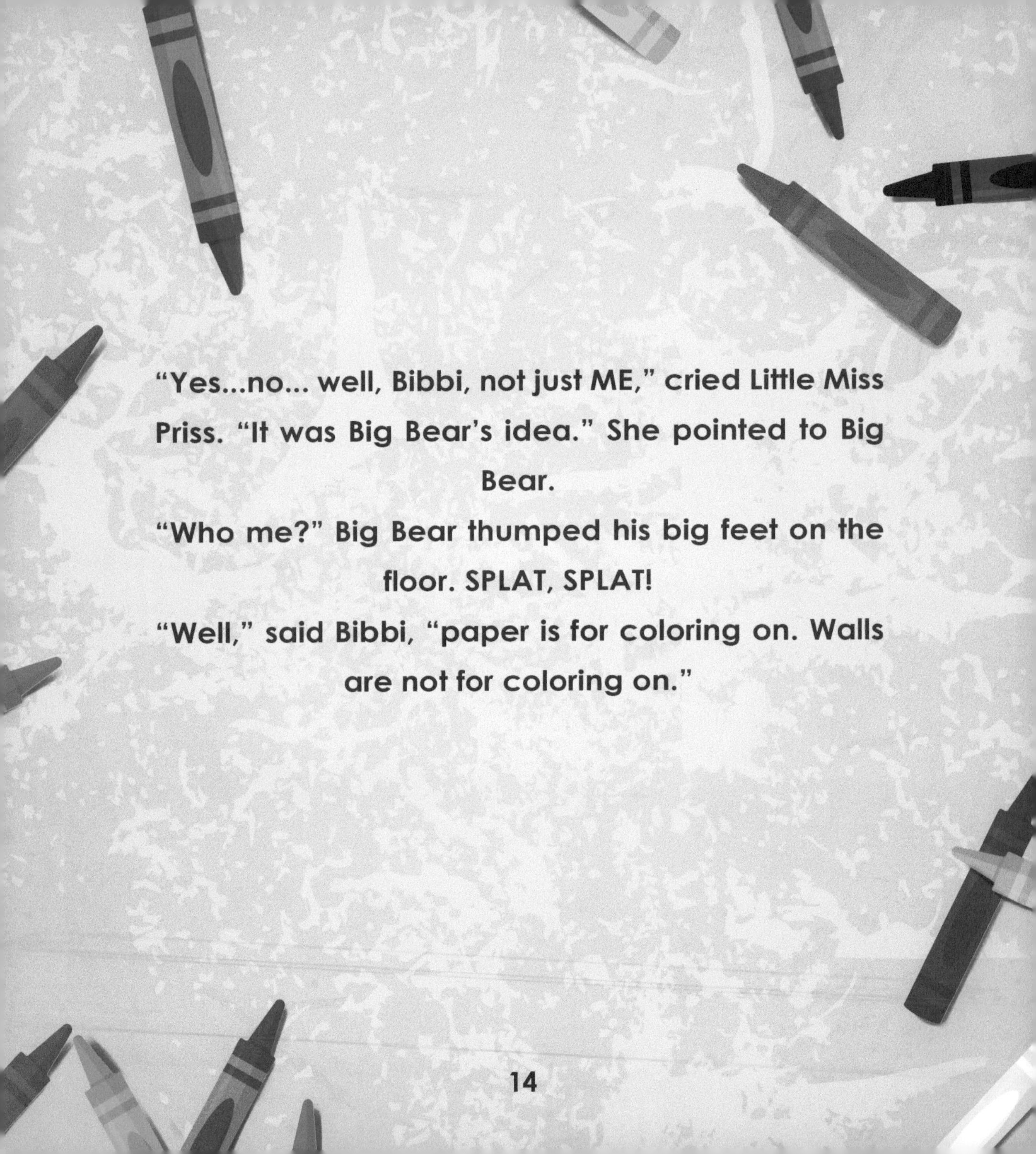

"Yes...no... well, Bibbi, not just ME," cried Little Miss Priss. "It was Big Bear's idea." She pointed to Big Bear.

"Who me?" Big Bear thumped his big feet on the floor. SPLAT, SPLAT!

"Well," said Bibbi, "paper is for coloring on. Walls are not for coloring on."

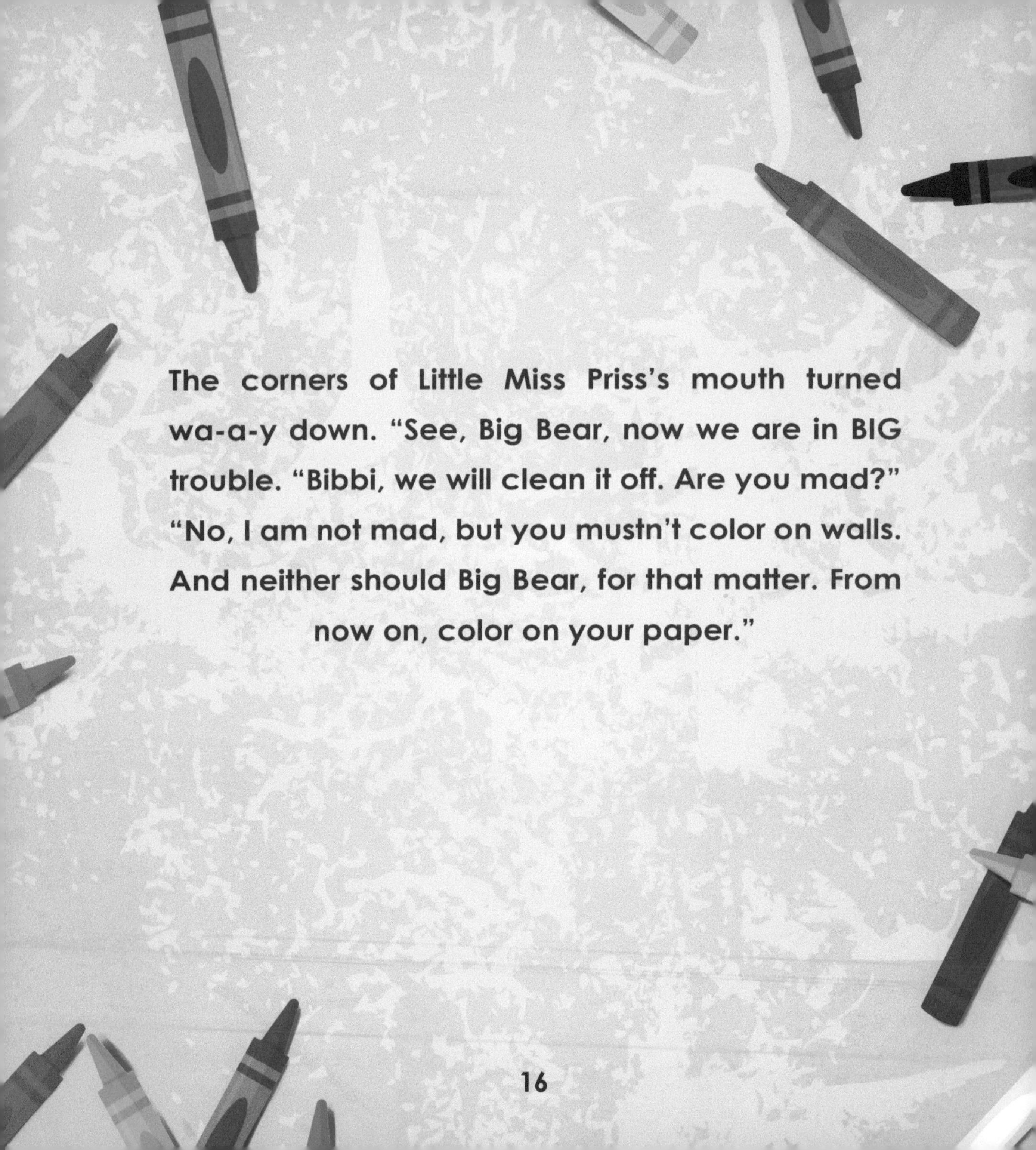

The corners of Little Miss Priss's mouth turned wa-a-y down. "See, Big Bear, now we are in BIG trouble. "Bibbi, we will clean it off. Are you mad?" "No, I am not mad, but you mustn't color on walls. And neither should Big Bear, for that matter. From now on, color on your paper."

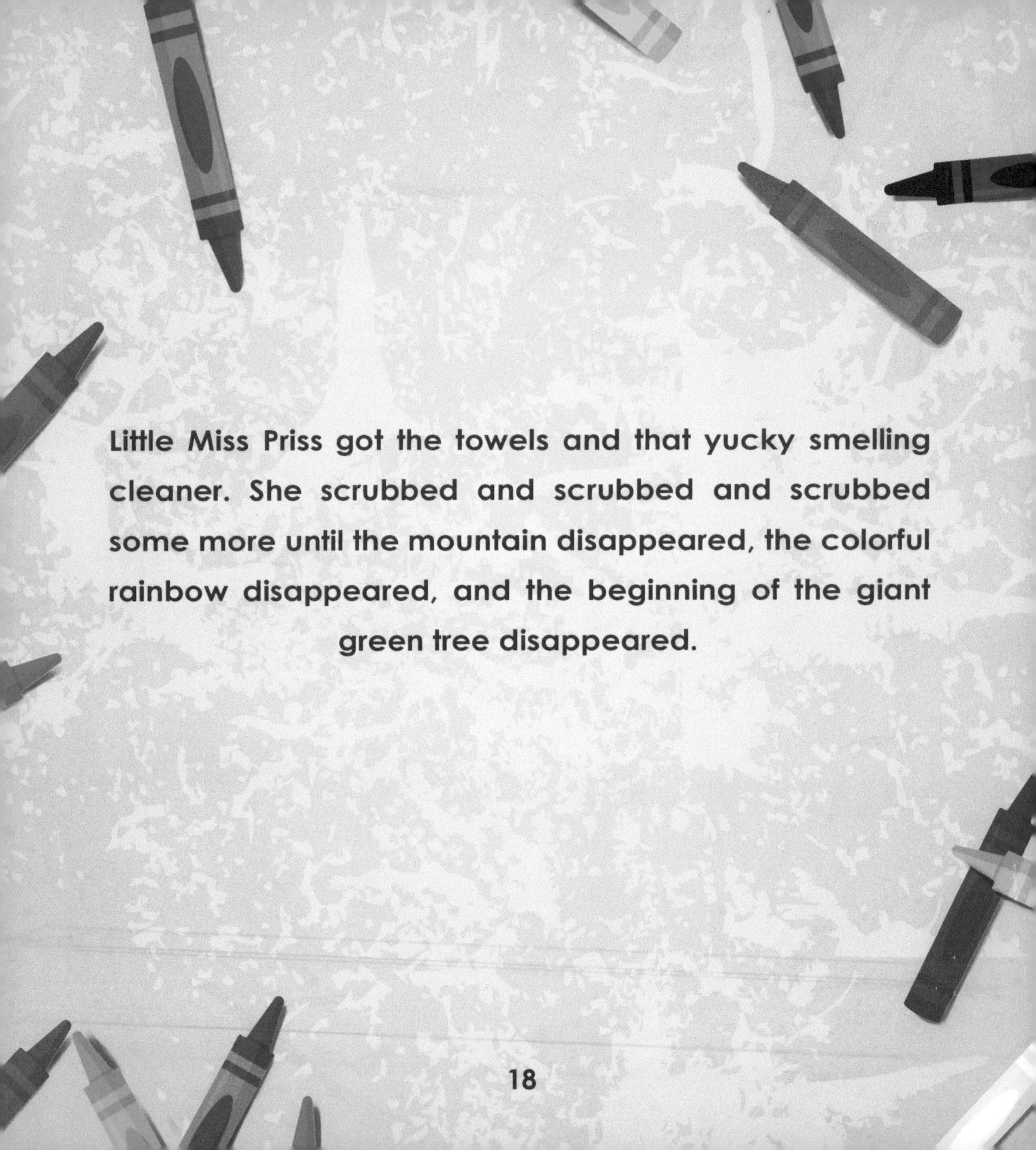

Little Miss Priss got the towels and that yucky smelling cleaner. She scrubbed and scrubbed and scrubbed some more until the mountain disappeared, the colorful rainbow disappeared, and the beginning of the giant green tree disappeared.

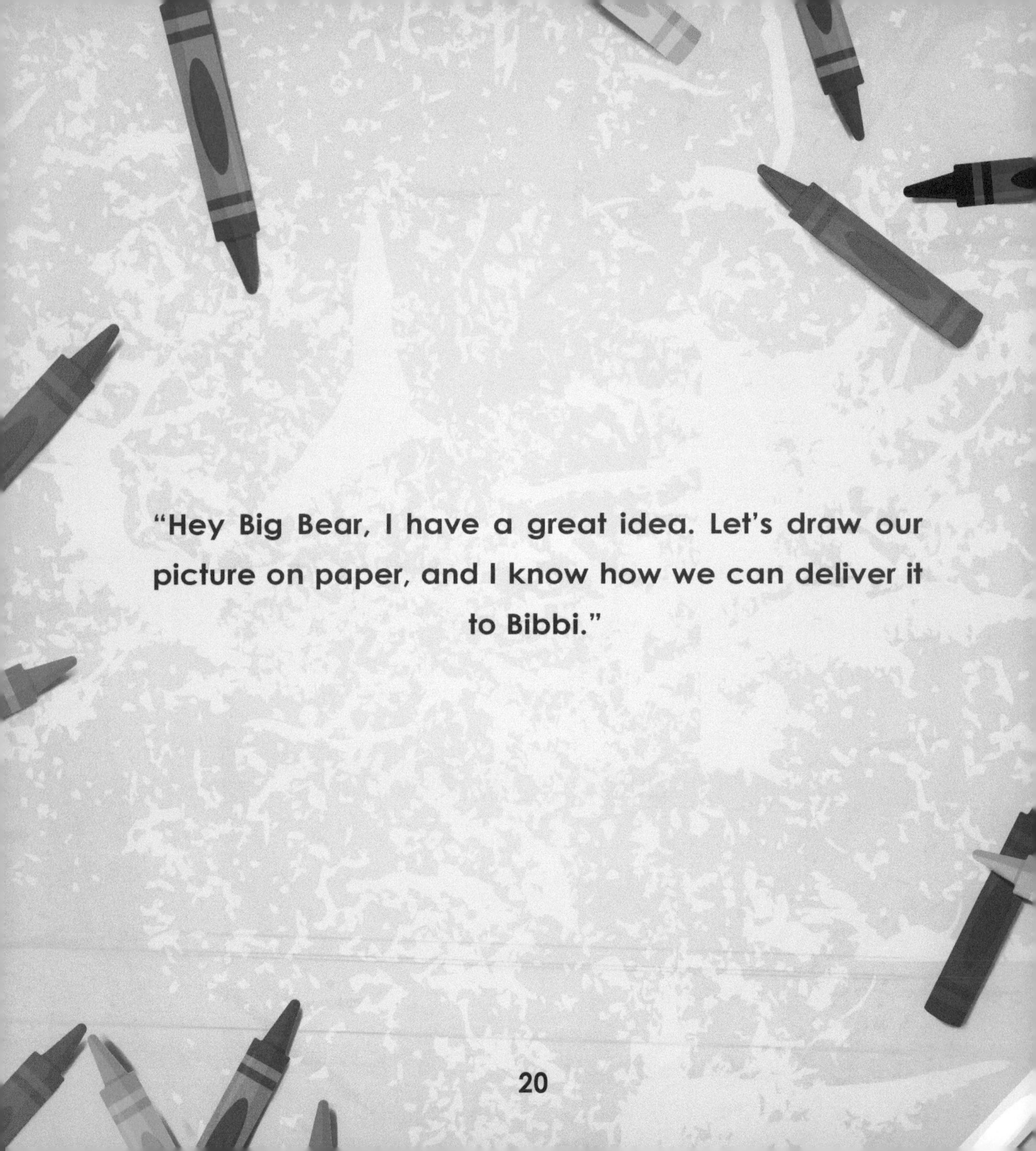

“Hey Big Bear, I have a great idea. Let’s draw our picture on paper, and I know how we can deliver it to Bibbi.”

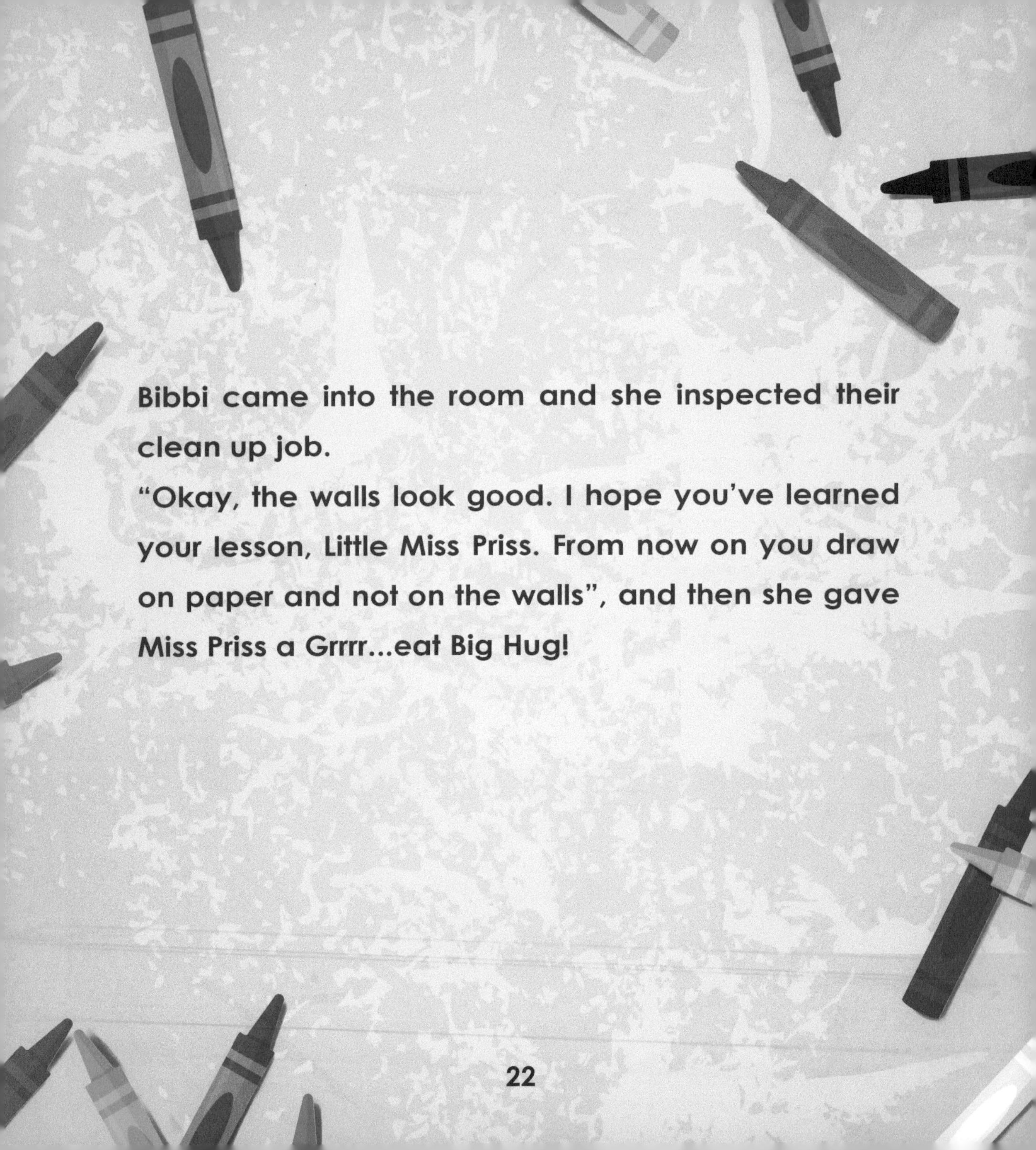

Bibbi came into the room and she inspected their clean up job.

"Okay, the walls look good. I hope you've learned your lesson, Little Miss Priss. From now on you draw on paper and not on the walls", and then she gave Miss Priss a Grrrr...eat Big Hug!

When she left the room, Big Bear and Little Miss Priss started on their new picture, but this time on paper.

When they were finished, Little Miss Priss drew an arrow on another piece of paper, got some tape, and went outside to the deck. There she taped the paper on the deck chair. Then she and Big Bear took rocks and spread them out on the way to the mailbox. Putting the picture into the mailbox, Little Miss Priss exclaimed, "This is like my story book of Hansel and Gretel."

They ran into the house and found Bibbi. "Bibbi, there is a surprise for you outside. Go to the deck and follow the arrow and rocks."

When Bibbi got to the mailbox, she opened it. There was the beautiful picture.

"Oh, Miss Priss, this is a beautiful picture and on paper instead of the wall. I will put this on my refrigerator when I get home. Granddaughters are the best. I love you very much." Little Miss Priss and Bibbi hugged each other with a BIG BEAR HUG.

THE END

Lightning Source UK Ltd.
Milton Keynes UK
UKHW051342220121
377491UK00004B/27
* 9 7 8 1 6 4 3 1 8 0 3 8 0 *